The Best Nest

By Doris L. Mueller

Illustrations by Sherry Neidigh

Long ago, when the world was young, only the magpie knew how to build a nest. Her nest was large and so well built that her babies were kept safe.

All the other birds laid their eggs here and there—on the ground, in a hollow log, or in a tree crotch. Their eggs were often stolen or lost, and the baby birds that did hatch were not safe from their enemies.

Poor baby birds! This made the mother birds very sad.

One day a mother bird said to her friend, "Let's ask Maggie Magpie to show us how to build a nest." So off they went to the magpie and said,

"We know how clever you are and that you have a strong nest to hold your eggs and protect your babies. We want to learn how to build a nest just like yours. Then our eggs and chicks will be safe too. Won't you please teach us?"

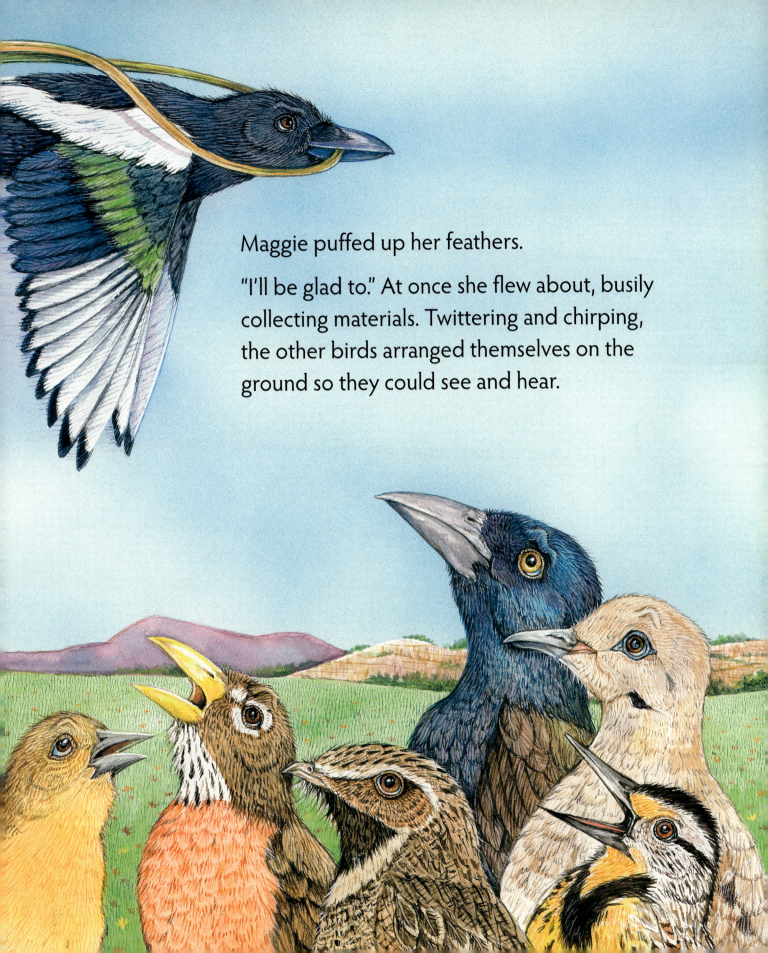

Maggie puffed up her feathers.

"I'll be glad to." At once she flew about, busily collecting materials. Twittering and chirping, the other birds arranged themselves on the ground so they could see and hear.

Maggie perched herself on a grassy mound and carefully smoothed the feathers in her beautiful long tail. She waited until the birds stopped their chattering.

"First of all," she began, "you must find a hollow space that is the right size."

"A hollow space—that's easy!" exclaimed the killdeer, lifting its head to show its sparkling black-and-white collar. Away it went, and the killdeer still lays its eggs in a hollow space on the ground.

"Pooh, who needs to build a nest?" whispered the whip-poor-will to the screech-owl. "Why not just gather leaves and lay our eggs on the ground?" The whip-poor-will, with whirring wings, flew away.

The screech-owl nodded wisely. "Who-o indeed? Or we can just use holes in trees."

"Ssh, we can't hear," scolded the birds near them. While Maggie waited for her class to settle down, the screech-owl flew off to find a tree hollow.

Maggie looked around to make sure the remaining birds were listening. "Next, you take some mud for an inside wall and place several twigs in it."

"Oh, I see," cried the blackbird, and she scurried away with a twig in her beak to look for a dab of mud. To this day, that's how blackbirds build their nests.

"But wait! We aren't finished," cried the frustrated magpie. "Don't you want to learn?" With a deep sigh, she turned back to her class.

"Then you make an outer wall of weeds or coarse grass." The starling flapped her wings excitedly. "I can do that! I can do that!" Away she flew to make her sloppy nest.

Trying to hide her annoyance, the magpie patted down a
layer of mud. Even before she could explain this step, the
grackle hurried off saying, "Oh, that'll be very cozy."

Maggie reminded her, "You must weave in more twigs or sticks to make sure the nest is strong."

"Twigs and sticks, twigs and sticks—that's good enough for me," warbled the meadowlark as it flew away. And the meadowlark builds a simple but sturdy nest to this day.

Maggie took some feathers to use as lining. "These will make your nest cozier."

"Oh yes," nodded the robin. "That's perfect," as she flicked her tail and flew off to build her nest.

Each time the magpie added something or explained a step, another bird would leave, not waiting for the lesson to finish. Maggie kept on teaching, but her voice become a bit shriller, her scowl a little deeper. Finally, she stopped to see if anyone had questions. But only two birds were left—the oriole and a silly dove who hadn't been listening. The dove cooed softly, "Take two, take two-o-o."

The magpie laid a twig in place and said, "No, one is enough." But the dove repeated, "Take two, take two-o-o." "I told you—one is enough," insisted Maggie.

The dove flapped her wings noisily and glided away, murmuring, "Take two, take two-o-o."

At last the magpie could stand no more. Angrily, she flew away and never again would she agree to teach the birds how to build nests.

But the oriole had listened carefully. She kept working and singing as she built a nest that was strong and beautiful—at least as beautiful as the magpie's.

And now you know why each bird builds its nest differently from every other bird.

For Creative Minds

Bird Fun Facts

Scientists sort animals into different classes. All the animals in this book are birds. While all birds have **feathers**, not all birds can fly (penguins do not fly). Birds **lay eggs**, **breathe air**, and are **warm blooded**.

Most birds build a nest that is hidden (**camouflaged**) or is hard for predators to reach. A nest may be made out of different things; you might even find dog hair or ribbons woven into nests.

male oriole

female oriole

Quite often **male** birds have bright feathers or coloring to attract a mate. It is usually the **female** who builds a nest, but sometimes the male or both male and female will build the nest together. Birds don't really need to learn how to build their nests; they are born knowing how (**instinct**).

Bird Math

Robins lay **two** broods of **three** to **six** eggs.

Screech Owls have only **one** brood a year but they lay between **two** and **seven** eggs, depending on the type of screech owl.

Killdeers have **one** or **two** broods a year with **three** to **five** eggs in each brood.

Which bird might lay the most eggs in a year? How many eggs? _____

Which bird might lay the fewest eggs in a year? How many eggs? _____

Why do you think birds have so many babies at a time? _____

Is it Injured?

If you see a fledgling on the ground, that does not mean it is injured or abandoned. It might just be learning how to fly or to find its own food. If it has no visible injury, you should keep pets away and leave it alone. Observe the bird from inside or far away so that the parent birds can reach it.

You should get help for the bird only if you can see a visible injury, you know for sure that the parents are dead, or the bird has been alone for over eight hours and it is now dark. It is illegal to care for migratory birds and most songbirds and you need to get the bird to an avian (bird) vet or a bird rehabilitator. Check the phone book or internet to find one in your area. Don't try to feed the bird.

Match the Nest Activity

Read the descriptions and match the nests to the correct birds.

1. ____

2. ____

3. ____

4. ____

5. ____

a. Magpie

The magpie builds a large bulky bowl of mud and grass surrounded by a latticework of sticks that point in all directions. The nest, which has a side entrance, is located high in trees.

b. Baltimore Oriole

The oriole carefully weaves a deep hanging pouch of plant fibers, hair, yarn, or string, and attaches it to a tree branch. This pouch, or sack, has a top opening. The nest is lined with hair, wool, or fine grasses. The female usually builds the nest while her mate stays nearby and sings. It can take from five to eight or more days to build this intricate nest.

c. Starling

This bird makes a sloppy nest. The male starts to build the nest in a hole in a tree or other opening, but the female often removes what he has done and adds her own materials. She fills the hole with grass, twigs, or dry leaves.

d. Common Grackle

The female builds a loose nest of weeds and grasses, with some help from her mate in the early stages. Sometimes she reinforces the nest with mud on the inside and lines it with grass or feathers.

e. Mourning Dove

This bird often finds a deserted nest, and the male brings sticks to the female to place in the nest. The female builds a careless platform of sticks with little, if any, lining of grass or weeds. The nest is so loosely made that it often falls apart in a storm.

6. ____

7. ____

8. ____

9 . ____

10. ____

11. ____

f. Whip-poor-will

This bird makes no nest; it lays its eggs on the ground on dead leaves.

g. Meadowlark

The female does all the work on the nest. First, she finds a depression in the ground that pleases her. She forms the base of the nest, lining it with coarse dry grasses and an inner lining of fine grasses. Then she builds a dome-shaped roof of grasses which she weaves into nearby plants.

h. Brewer's Blackbird

Her nest is on the ground, in shrubs, or in trees. She uses twigs or grasses made stronger with mud or cow dung.

i. Robin

The robin builds her nest early in the spring and may place it in an evergreen shrub or tree fork. Her nest is a deep cup, which she shapes by sitting in it and pressing her breast against the edges. The nest is made of grass, weed stalks, and strips of cloth or string worked into soft mud. It is lined with fine grass.

j. Screech-owl

The female lays her eggs in anatural opening or a hole in a tree.

k. Killdeer

The male scrapes several hollows in an open stretch of ground, and the female chooses one of them. She adds a few pebbles and bits of grass or woodchips to line the depression.

Answers: 1j; 2h; 3f; 4b; 5i; 6d; 7e; 8a; 9k; 10c; 11g

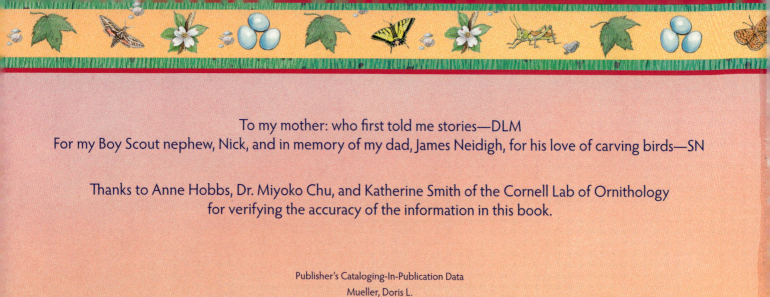

To my mother: who first told me stories—DLM
For my Boy Scout nephew, Nick, and in memory of my dad, James Neidigh, for his love of carving birds—SN

Thanks to Anne Hobbs, Dr. Miyoko Chu, and Katherine Smith of the Cornell Lab of Ornithology
for verifying the accuracy of the information in this book.

Publisher's Cataloging-In-Publication Data

Mueller, Doris L.
The best nest / by Doris L. Mueller ; illustrated by Sherry Neidigh.
p. : col. ill. ; cm.

Summary: In this retelling of an old English folktale featuring birds native
to the U.S., Magpie patiently explains to the other birds how to build a nest.
Some birds are impatient and fly off without listening to all the directions,
however, and that is why, to this day, birds' nests come in all different shapes and sizes.
Includes "For Creative Minds" section.

Interest age level: 004-008.
Interest grade level: P-3.
ISBN: 978-1-934359-09-9 (hardcover)
ISBN: 978-1-934359-25-9 (pbk.)

1. Birds--Nests--Juvenile fiction. 2. Magpies--Juvenile fiction.
3. Listening--Juvenile fiction. 4. Birds--Nests--Fiction.
5. Magpies--Fiction. 6. Listening--Fiction. 7. Folklore. I. Neidigh, Sherry. II. Title.

PZ8.1.M84 Be 2008

398.24/52/8256 [E]   2007935084

Lexile Level 510

Printed in China

Sylvan Dell Publishing
976 Houston Northcutt Blvd., Suite 3
Mt. Pleasant, SC 29464

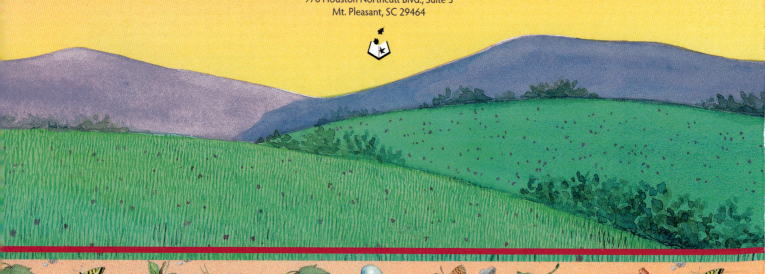